ROAD TRIP MONSTERS

Race for First Place

DISCARDED

by Candice Ransom
illustrated by Tyrell Solomon

Ready-to-Read

Simon Spotlight

New York   London   Toronto   Sydney   New Delhi

To Wyatt, Tate, Abe, and Nik —C. R.

To my mother, Tiffany —T. S.

SIMON SPOTLIGHT

An imprint of Simon & Schuster Children's Publishing Division

1230 Avenue of the Americas, New York, New York 10020

This Simon Spotlight edition May 2022

Text copyright © 2022 by Candice Ransom

Illustrations copyright © 2022 by Tyrell Solomon

SIMON SPOTLIGHT, READY-TO-READ, and colophon are registered trademarks of Simon & Schuster, Inc.

For information about special discounts for bulk purchases, please contact Simon & Schuster Special Sales at 1-866-506-1949 or business@simonandschuster.com.

Manufactured in the United States of America 0322 LAK

2 4 6 8 10 9 7 5 3 1

Library of Congress Cataloging-in-Publication Data

Names: Ransom, Candice F., 1952– author. | Solomon, Tyrell, illustrator. Title: Race for first place / by Candice Ransom ; illustrated by Tyrell Solomon. Description: New York : Simon Spotlight, 2022. | Series: Red truck monsters ; #1 | Summary: "A family of monsters enters its red truck into a monster truck race, but will it win first place?"—Provided by publisher. Identifiers: LCCN 2021027934 (print) | LCCN 2021027935 (ebook) | ISBN 9781665901673 (pb) | ISBN 9781665901680 (hc) | ISBN 9781665901697 (ebook) | Subjects: CYAC: Stories in rhyme. | Monsters—Fiction. | Trucks—Fiction. | Monster trucks—Fiction. | Truck racing—Fiction. | LCGFT: Stories in rhyme. Classification: LCC PZ8.3.R1467 Rac 2022 (print) | LCC PZ8.3.R1467 (ebook) | DDC [E]—dc23 LC record available at https://lccn.loc.gov/2021027934 LC ebook record available at https://lccn.loc.gov/2021027935

Monsters need
a brand-new ride.

Something roomy,
tall inside.

Sporty car?
No place to sit.

Spiffy red truck?
Perfect fit!

They see cows,
a grocery store.

Plain old
highway.
Such a bore.

Monsters high-five.
Monsters grin.
Monsters hope
their truck might win.

Good idea?
Not so much.

So many trucks!
Twenty-two!
Purple, yellow,
black, and blue.

One whopping truck
called Meatball.
Last one is Red,
smallest of all.

Along the track,
engines *vroom*.

The green lights flash.
Drivers zoom!

Meatball's tires
turn round and round,
digging circles
in the ground.

Trusty Red
is not too late.
Its wheels draw
a figure eight.

Meatball looms.
"He cannot pass!"
"Lay some rubber!"
"Hit the gas!"

"Ramp straight ahead.
Hang on tight!"
Red grabs big air,
like a kite.

Next Red does
a tricky flip.
Monster tummies
twist and tip.

Other trucks
are stalled and stuck.
Bumpers fly off.
Monsters duck!

Red jolts over
ruts and holes.
Bolts break loose,
but Red still rolls.

Two trucks left.
Red plus the pro.
Neck and neck.
One stunt to go. . . .

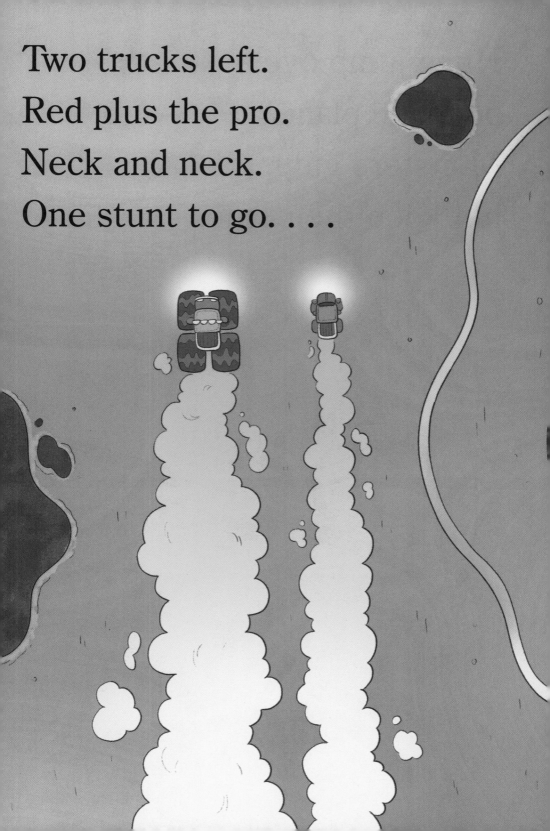

Huge jump over
boat and plane!
Monsters gulp
but keep their lane.

Hothead Meatball
nudges Red.
Its back wheel slips,
loses tread.

Angry crowd leaps
to their feet.
"Unfair!"
"Bad sport!"
"What a cheat!"

Meatball speeds
but lands on the boat.
Giant truck down!
Judge takes note.

Monsters swallow,
take a chance.

Front wheels slap down.
Watch Red dance!

Revved-up Red
sails like a spear.

Pushes Meatball
in the clear!

Both land safe
with space to spare.
Both win grand prize
as a pair.

Hungry drivers
want to eat.
Enough for all!
Winner's treat.

Monsters gain
some friends and fame.
Happy for roads . . .
nice and tame.